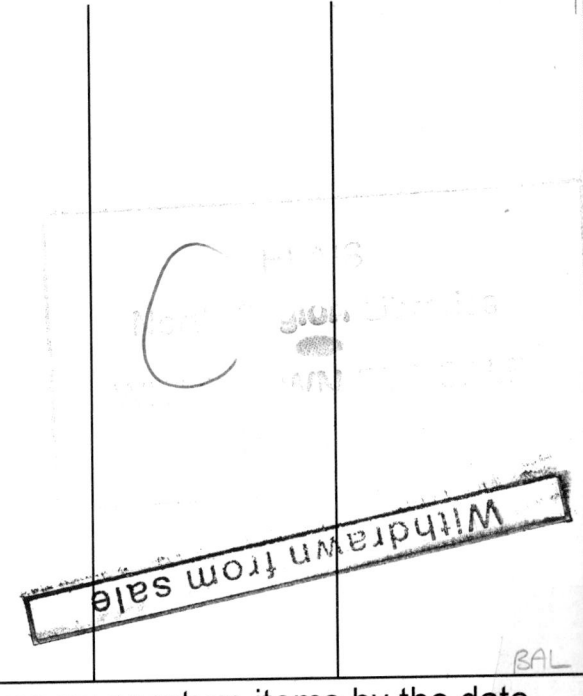

BAL

Please renew or return items by the date shown on your receipt

www.hertsdirect.org/libraries

Renewals and enquiries:

0300 123 4049

Textphone for hearing or speech impaired

0300 123 4041

Hertfordshire

D1472001

525 032 59 1

To Iver and Maeve Babich — AF

To my big brother, Foxy McFoxFace — EF

STRIPES PUBLISHING
An imprint of the Little Tiger Group
1 The Coda Centre, 189 Munster Road,
London SW6 6AW

A paperback original
First published in Great Britain in 2016

Text copyright © Adam Frost, 2016
Illustrations copyright © Emily Fox, 2016
Back cover images courtesy of www.shutterstock.com

ISBN: 978-1-84715-726-3

A CIP catalogue record for this book is available
from the British Library.

Printed and bound in the UK.

10 9 8 7 6 5 4 3 2 1

Fox Investigates

A Trail of Trickery

ADAM FROST
ILLUSTRATED BY EMILY FOX

Stripes

THE CURTAIN RISES

Wily Fox, the world's greatest detective, was outside the Griffin Theatre in London, staring up at a poster. It was 2 p.m. on a Tuesday afternoon. Usually a matinee performance would have just started, but not today. As the poster said, today's performance of *Escape from Spooky Manor* was cancelled.

Wily went round to the stage door and knocked. The theatre caretaker – an ancient mongoose wearing about nine layers of clothes – opened the door.

"Ah, Wily Fox. Roderick Rabbit said you were coming. Who'd have thought it? An actual ghost! Here at the Griffin!"

"Apparently so," said Wily, stepping inside.

"I mean, actors have claimed to see ghosts here before," the mongoose said, leading Wily down some steps. "The Headless Hyena, for example. The See-through Sheep. But a ghost has never appeared on stage before. In front of an audience!"

The mongoose ushered Wily through a set of double doors and into the stalls, where a rabbit was sitting in the first row of seats, biting his nails and murmuring to himself. He was wearing a long red scarf and a paisley waistcoat. He leaped up.

"Mr Fox," the rabbit exclaimed, "thank you SO much for coming!" He embraced Wily, giving him a kiss on both cheeks.

Wily stiffened and cleared his throat. "No problem," he said.

The mongoose disappeared and the rabbit began his story.

"My name is Roderick Aloysius Rabbit and I am producer and director of *Escape from Spooky Manor* – a spine-chilling, nerve-shredding journey into your deepest, darkest fears."

"I don't scare easily," said Wily.

"This may test your courage," said Roderick. "Allow me to set the scene."

The rabbit bounded up on to the stage. Behind him was an elaborate set: the entrance hall of a huge manor house.

"So on Saturday night, all was proceeding as normal. It was the end of the final act – the ghost's last appearance. The actors were assembled on THIS side of the stage." Roderick sprang across to the left-hand side of the stage. "Gloria Gerbil says her line: 'Perhaps we are finally free of this turbulent spirit', there is a rumble of thunder, a flash of lightning and on walks the ghost."

Roderick pointed to the door on the other side of the set.

"This is usually Vladimir Vole in a suit of armour," said Roderick, "but on Saturday night, it was a glowing shroud, hovering above the ground. It gave an ear-piercing shriek and then disappeared."

"Weird," Wily said.

"At first the actors kept going," said Roderick. "They assumed it was Vladimir, trying out a different costume. He takes his performances VERY seriously. Then, at the end of the show, they found him in a cupboard in his dressing room. Hiding. The ghost had appeared to him backstage, then taken his place in the scene. After that, the actors refused to go on the following night."

"Did you search the theatre?"

"Of course," said Roderick, "but there was no sign of the ghost. It had come from nowhere and vanished without a trace."

"So it was just a practical joke," said Wily.

"But who? Why?" Roderick protested. "I have no enemies. I LOVE everyone. Besides, the actors say the ghost looked so REAL. They're superstitious at the best of times. Now they're saying the play is CURSED."

"Well, I don't believe in curses – or ghosts," said Wily.

"Maybe you're right," said Roderick, "but I have to say, they've convinced ME. A dark shadow has fallen over this production – and it's going to bankrupt me!"

"So what do you need me to do?" Wily asked.

"Find the ghost, of course," said Roderick. "I've had to cancel today's performance. I can probably afford to cancel a few more. But Saturday! I must re-open on Saturday! Or all my money will be gone! My reputation – gone! Find the ghost by Saturday, Mr Fox, and send it back to where it came from!"

He buried his head in his arm and burst into tears.

Wily climbed up on to the stage and handed Roderick a handkerchief.

"You're very kind," said Roderick, blowing his nose loudly. "There is one consolation.

I made my actors promise not to tell anyone about this. Obviously if the public found out that the theatre was haunted, they might not come either."

"Can you rely on your actors to keep the secret?" Wily asked.

"For now," said Roderick, "but that's another reason I need this ghost found quickly. Actors love to gossip."

Wily glanced around the theatre. "You know I'm a detective, right? Not a ghost hunter."

"Most ghost hunters are fakes," replied Roderick. "They're actors playing a part. I know the type a mile off. I need a proper detective. Someone who can solve mysteries."

Wily nodded and started to inspect the stage. "Let's see if your ghost really did vanish without a trace," he said.

He walked over to where Roderick said the

ghost had appeared.

"Has anything been moved since Saturday night?" Wily asked.

"Unfortunately yes," said Roderick. "I wasn't really thinking. We put all the props backstage and the caretaker swept the boards."

Wily took out his magnifying glass and squatted down. Then he searched the stage floor, looking for hairs, fingerprints, threads of clothing. There was nothing.

"Shame the caretaker's so good at his job," Wily muttered.

As he searched, Wily wondered about Roderick's story. He tried to keep an open mind about ghosts. There was no proof that they DID exist, but there was no proof that they DIDN'T.

Which type would this ghost be – real or pretend?

Then he spotted something glinting in between the floorboards.

He crouched down and looked through his magnifying glass. There, in between two of the boards, was a wisp of bright white fabric. Wily tugged on the end and pulled it out. The moment he held it up to the light, it turned black.

"Maybe your ghost did leave something behind," Wily said.

"What is it?" Roderick asked.

"I'm not sure," said Wily, "but you can only see it in the dark."

He cupped his hand round the material and it glowed white again.

"Wow," Roderick gulped, "do you think it came from the … afterlife?"

"Hmm," said Wily. "I think it came from the shops."

Wily dropped the material into a small plastic bag. "I'll ask my friend Albert to analyze it."

Wily then lifted up a rug in the centre of the stage and revealed a trap door.

"That dates back to Victorian times," said

Roderick. "I don't think the mechanism works any more."

"Well, it's been used recently," Wily said. "The dust round the edge has been disturbed."

Wily opened the trap door and leaped into the small dark room below. He peered into the trap-door mechanism.

"It looks like the cogs have just been oiled," Wily called to Roderick.

"Not by any of us," Roderick shouted back.

"This ghost is either very resourceful," said Wily, jumping up on to the stage, "or he has a helper here on earth."

Wily climbed up a ladder on the side of the stage and examined the lighting rig.

He looked at the stage lighting plan for "Act Three: Ghost's Entrance".

It looked like this:

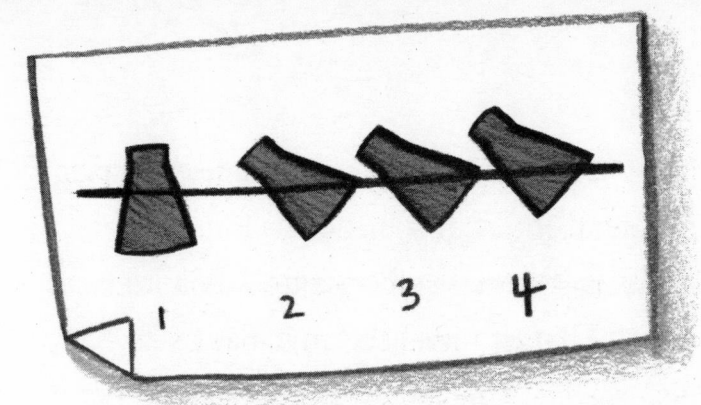

However the lights on the rig were positioned like this:

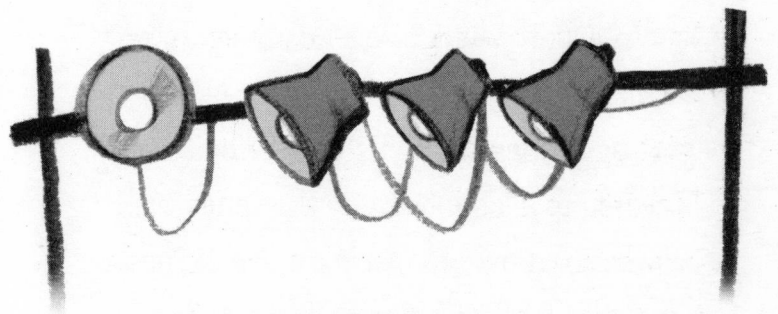

"Has anyone changed these lights since Saturday night?" Wily shouted down.

"No!" Roderick shouted back. "The stagehands have refused to come back, too."

So, Wily thought to himself, at the end of

the third act, the ghost was meant to be under the spotlights. But someone had moved the lights so they were all pointing AWAY from the ghost. This kept the actor in darkness.

"Who was up here working the lights on Saturday night?" Wily asked, as he climbed down the ladder.

"No one," said Roderick. "They're all programmed in advance. We just press a button on that console over there at the start of the show. Then the lights move themselves." He pointed to a large board in the wings.

Wily walked over to inspect it. He pulled out his magnifying glass again and saw, between two of the sliders, another tangle of glowing fabric. He pulled it out and dropped it in his evidence bag.

"Looks like there was a manual override," Wily said. "Now, you said you had no enemies?"

Roderick blinked. "I can't think of any."

"What about the actors?" Wily asked. "Do they have enemies?"

"I suppose other actors can get quite jealous of Vladimir," said Roderick, "because he's the most famous, you see."

"It's interesting that the ghost didn't just scare him – he also replaced him on stage," said Wily. "Time to pay Vladimir a visit, I think."

"So you have a hunch?" Roderick asked anxiously. "You can solve the case by Saturday night?"

Wily nodded and patted Roderick's shoulder. "The criminal doesn't have a ghost of a chance."

WILY GETS SPOOKED

Wily was standing in Albert Mole's laboratory, looking at a bank of computer screens. Albert was Wily's loyal assistant and his laboratory was deep underground – over one hundred metres below Wily's office.

"So you've checked Roderick, Vladimir, the other actors and the stagehands?" asked Wily.

"Yep," said Albert. "No criminal records, no suspicious activities."

"What about phone records?"

"They've only phoned friends and relatives,"

said Albert. "No unusual numbers."

"Then who's doing this?" Wily muttered to himself.

"Well, er, Wily," said Albert, "I don't mean to worry you, but it COULD be a ghost."

"The clues don't point that way," said Wily. "Someone reprogrammed a lighting rig. And left glowing fabric behind."

"I know," said Albert, "I'm analyzing the material now. But in case you *are* dealing with a supernatural organism, I've made these..."

He opened a drawer in his desk and revealed a bag of grey pellets and a laser gun.

Wily picked up the bag of pellets.

"Those are fortified smoke bombs," said Albert. "If you need to escape fast, they'll release a small tornado."

"And this?" Wily asked, taking the laser gun.

"It's a fast-acting particle freezer," said Albert.

"It turns anything that moves into ice. It works on gases, so I think it should work on ghosts, too. Blue button is freeze, red button is thaw. Test it on that," Albert said, pointing at a beetle that was crawling on the floor.

Wily pressed the blue button on the handle of the gun. There was a humming noise, then a zigzag of blue light shot out of the barrel and the beetle froze. Crackling ice crystals spread across its body.

"Now thaw," said Albert.

Wily pressed the red button on the handle, a jagged crimson laser shot out of the barrel and the beetle skittered off.

As they watched the beetle go, Roderick's photo appeared on all of Albert's screens.

"He's calling the emergency number," said Albert. "It must be serious."

"Answer it," said Wily.

Roderick had tears in his eyes as he spoke. "I've got reporters at my front door," he wailed. "Someone must have told the newspapers."

"OK," said Wily, "stay calm. If they ask you anything, just say, 'No comment'."

"This is EXACTLY what I was afraid of," said Roderick, his ears twitching. "EVERYONE is going to think the theatre is haunted."

"I'm on the case," said Wily. "I'll find out who the ghost is and tell the whole world the truth."

After saying goodbye to Roderick, Wily turned to Albert. "Find out who broke the story," he said.

Albert pressed a button and each of his screens displayed a different website or TV show. He scanned the monitors for every single mention of the Griffin Theatre.

After a few seconds Albert said, "Here," and pointed at the website of the *Daily Smear*.

"Story published at 4 p.m. this afternoon," said Albert, "before anyone else."

"Check the actors' phone records again," said Wily. "See if any of them contacted the *Smear*."

Wily read the first part of the article. It was by a journalist called Pete Pigeon.

DAILY SMEAR

There were chilling scenes at the Griffin Theatre on Saturday night when the audience for *Escape from Spooky Manor* were subjected to a real-life horror show! At the end of the third act, star actor Vladimir Vole, who is winning rave reviews for his performance as the 'Castle Ghost', was replaced on stage by a real-life spook! The ghost first appeared to Vladimir Vole in his dressing room, passing through two walls and a locked door.

"None of the actors made any calls this afternoon," said Albert.

"Hmm," said Wily, "so how did Pete Pigeon find out about the ghost? SOMEONE must have told him. But who – and why?"

"Maybe the ghost visited him, too," Albert said.

25

"Maybe," said Wily, putting the smoke pellets and the particle freezer in the inside pocket of his coat. "But we should start by finding out everything we can about Pete Pigeon. And as for Vladimir, now I REALLY want to talk to him. He's just become a key suspect."

"Why?"

"Look at the last paragraph of the news story. 'The ghost first appeared to Vladimir Vole in his dressing room, passing through two walls and a locked door'!" said Wily. "How did Pete Pigeon know this? Vladimir was the only person in the dressing room. So either HE told Pete – or he told someone else and THEY did."

Albert nodded.

"Either way," said Wily, "he has questions to answer."

Vladimir's flat was a five-minute taxi ride from Wily's office. As Wily was being driven through the evening mist, he spotted a newsagent's on the corner. The board outside read: GHOST STEALS THE SHOW. On the next corner, there was an electronics shop. The TVs in the window were all showing the news: STAGE FRIGHT AT THE GRIFFIN THEATRE. The story was everywhere.

Vladimir's flat was on the ground floor of a building just behind the British Museum. Wily knocked on his door and waited.

"Who is it?" asked a scared voice.

"Wily Fox," said Wily. "I'm a detective."

"How do I know you're not a ghost?" said the voice behind the door.

Wily held up his detective's badge to the peephole in the middle of the door. "Ghosts don't carry these."

There was a moment of silence. Then Wily heard one bolt after another being slid across and a chain being rattled backwards.

A short plump vole opened the door a fraction, peered at Wily and then beckoned him inside.

Wily found himself in a small one-bedroomed flat. The walls were covered with photos of Vladimir performing in different plays. In the corner, there was a large oak wardrobe. The door was open and there was a mattress stuffed into it.

"Strange place to sleep," said Wily.

"I feel safest in there at the moment," said Vladimir.

"Can't ghosts walk through wardrobe doors as well?" Wily asked.

Vladimir froze, as if he hadn't thought of this before.

"It's OK," added Wily quickly. "What you saw wasn't a ghost. I need you to help me find out who it was."

Wily looked Vladimir up and down. He seemed genuinely scared. It didn't look as if he was involved in a crime or a conspiracy. But then again – Vladimir was an actor, so he would be good at pretending.

"Tell me exactly what happened that evening," said Wily.

"OK." Vladimir gulped. "I was in my dressing room, doing my stretches and my vocal exercises. Suddenly the lights were switched off. I didn't hear anyone open or close the door, so I don't know how it got in. I turned round and there it was. A large glowing shape with red eyes. It emitted a horrifying shriek. And then it reached out a claw towards me."

Vladimir was shaking and sweat appeared on his forehead.

"A claw?" Wily asked.

"Yes, like the hand of a skeleton. But black."

"And then?"

"I'd seen enough," said Vladimir. "I leaped into the cupboard."

"Who else have you told?" asked Wily.

"Nobody. Gloria Gerbil – she's the leading lady – came in and found me, but I didn't tell her anything about what had happened."

"Why not?"

"Didn't Roderick tell you?" said Vladimir. "I was too frightened to speak. I nodded when

Gloria asked me if I'd seen a ghost, but that's all. I haven't said a word to anyone since. Well, not until I started talking to you."

Vladimir mopped his brow with a handkerchief. "I must say, I feel a lot safer now you're on the case."

Suddenly the room went dark. Vladimir shrieked.

"It's OK," Wily whispered.

"It's back!" Vladimir screamed.

In one corner of the room, a glowing shape materialized. Its body was a white cloak with two small red eyes at the top. There was smoke around its feet, which made it look as if it was hovering above the floor. It moved slowly towards Wily and pointed at him with a bony talon. Then it gave a blood-curdling shriek that made the fur on the back of Wily's neck stand up.

"I wondered when you'd show up!" Wily growled and pulled the particle freezer out of his coat pocket.

The ghost seemed to realize he was under attack, because a cane appeared from within its cloak. Wily ducked as the cane was swung towards him. Then he pressed the blue button on his particle freezer. A bolt shot out of the end, hitting the wall behind the ghost and leaving a patch of ice.

The ghost gave another high-pitched

shriek and fled, with Wily in pursuit, firing off another blast from his particle freezer as he went. The ghost lashed out with its cane again, striking Wily on the arm.

"You're pretty lively for a dead guy," Wily snarled.

Wily followed the ghost into the square, but when they got outside, he stopped dead. The London mist had become fog. He could see three glowing shapes, but which should he chase? They were all moving in different directions.

Wily whipped out his spyphone and opened the binoculars app. He zoomed in on the first glowing shape – it was the headlight of a motorbike. The second shape was an old otter shining a torch as she tottered home. He zoomed in on the third shape – but it vanished before he got a proper look.

Wily ran in that direction and soon a glowing light appeared in front of him. The outline of the animal's body, the way it moved – it had to be the ghost.

Wily ran after it.

It turned a corner, so did Wily. For a second, he almost lost it as more glowing lights appeared in the fog – the yellow halo of a street lamp and the red glow of a bike light. But he kept his eyes fixed on the ghostly blur.

He was seconds away when the light

disappeared. He was alone in the fog, listening for the slightest sound.

Suddenly the light reared up in front of him, almost blinding him. The ghost must have been hiding behind a car or wall. The cane struck him again.

Wily staggered backwards, then clenched his teeth and dived forwards. He grabbed hold of something hard and yanked it. It was a briefcase.

The ghost tugged it, too, refusing to let go.

"Do you mind if I inspect your bag, sir?" Wily growled.

Then something gave way and paper went everywhere.

Ghosts don't usually carry documents around, Wily said to himself.

As the ghost tried to gather up the documents, Wily pulled out his particle freezer. The ghost emitted another ear-splitting shriek and lashed out with its cane. Just as Wily pulled the trigger, the cane knocked him out cold. The last thing Wily saw was a blue bolt zipping out of his particle freezer. Then everything went black.

WILY TAKES TO THE SKIES

When Wily came round, he was propped up in an armchair in Albert's lab.

He sprang to his feet. "What happened?"

"It's OK," said Albert, "you just slept off the bump to the head. It's Wednesday afternoon."

"But ... how did you find me?"

"I built a chip into the particle freezer so I know where it is at all times," said Albert. "The signal went dead so I knew something had happened." He gestured at his workbench, where the slightly bent particle freezer was sitting next to a set of tools. "You dropped it when you got knocked out."

"Blast!" Wily snarled. "I thought I hit him with it just before he whacked me."

"You didn't hit him," said Albert, "but you did hit THIS." He held up a sheaf of papers encased in ice. "I don't think our ghost spotted them in the fog." Albert tapped his thick glasses. "But I saw them."

Wily took the papers and smiled. "Well done, Albert. They must have fallen out of his briefcase when it sprang open."

He peered through the layer of ice that distorted the words on the pages inside.

"Let's thaw these out," Wily said.

"Give me two more minutes," Albert said. He hammered and wrestled with the broken particle freezer, finally handing it over to Wily with a grin. "Good as new."

Wily pointed the particle freezer at the bundle of paper and pressed the "thaw" button.

A red bolt shot out of the end of the barrel and the papers started to glow. Within a couple of seconds, they were dry.

The first sheet read:

Instruct PP: Wednesday, 17.00, 51.5033° N, 0.1197° W

"They're coordinates, Albert," Wily said. "Look 'em up."

Under this first sheet, there was a holiday brochure from Hapgood Hotels.

Wily flicked through the first few pages. "Why would the ghost be carrying a hotel brochure?" he said out loud. "Maybe he's staying at one of these hotels. Or he has done in the past."

Wily kept flicking through the brochure. "They specialize in hotels for nocturnal animals," he continued. "Lights go out from 9 a.m. to 5 p.m. Breakfast is at seven in the evening and lunch at midnight."

"So our villain's nocturnal?" Albert asked.

"He could be," said Wily. "After all, every time he's appeared so far, it's been dark outside."

Albert nodded, then glanced at one of his computer screens. "Those coordinates are for the London Eye." Albert rubbed his chin. "That's an odd place to meet. Pretty public."

Wily pondered this for a second and then said, "Unless they're meeting ON the London Eye rather than AT it."

He looked again at the sheet of paper.

Instruct PP: Wednesday, 17.00,
51.5033° N, 0.1197° W

"He says he's instructing PP – I wonder who or what PP is."

"Not sure," said Albert.

"And it says Wednesday at five o'clock." Wily looked at his watch. "Albert, it's 4.15 p.m. now. I've got to dash!"

"OK, OK, but before you go," said Albert. "Er ... I wasn't sure whether to give you this – it's still a prototype, but if you're going to be racing round the London Eye, you may need to be airborne."

He handed Wily a small disc that was a bit like a hockey puck.

"Press your thumb in the middle, place it on the floor and stand back."

Wily did exactly this and watched as the disc sprouted huge wings and a fibreglass frame.

"A hang-glider!" Wily exclaimed, lifting it off the ground.

It was so light, he was able to balance it on his finger.

"Yes, but it's more than that! It can take off from ground level, too," Albert said.

"Really?" Wily asked.

"Yes, it's like a kite," said Albert. "As long as you're running fast enough, wind will rush under the fabric and lift you off the ground."

"Neat," said Wily. "And how do I put it away?"

"That button there," said Albert.

Wily pressed the button, the hang-glider started to shake and then it collapsed back down into a tiny disc. Wily dropped it into his trouser pocket and patted it.

"Better fly," he said.

Half an hour later, Wily was standing at the bottom of the London Eye. Once again, he pulled out his spyphone and opened the binoculars app. He looked from one pod to the next. Most of the cabins were full of tourists – animals with cameras and guidebooks and flowery shirts. One booth contained a school party that seemed to be trying to break the world record for most animals stuffed into a confined space. Noses and paws were squished up against the windows while the teacher in the middle tried to stop everyone fighting.

Then Wily saw a cabin near the top of the Eye with just two animals inside. One was definitely a pigeon. The other was tall and thin, but its face and body were obscured by a thick black cloak with a hood.

Wily remembered the letters in the message – "Instruct PP". Someone Pigeon? Then in a flash he remembered the news article in the *Daily Smear* from the day before – written by Pete Pigeon.

Ideas flooded into his mind. This animal could have haunted the theatre and then told Pete Pigeon what had happened. Vladimir Vole said he hadn't spoken to anyone since the haunting. Which left the ghost. Only the ghost knew the details. So had the ghost given Pete the story? And was he now up there in that pod giving Pete another story?

Wily needed to get to that cabin.

He looked at the queue for the London Eye. There were at least a hundred animals standing in line.

He glanced up at the cabin. If he waited for them to get back down he'd have missed everything. He thought about using the hang-glider, but they'd see him coming a mile off. He needed a different strategy.

He remembered the extra-strong smoke pellets that Albert had given him. They were meant to cover his tracks when he was escaping, but perhaps he could put them to another use.

He looked at the large generator at the bottom of the London Eye, checked that nobody was looking and then tossed a pellet at it. Smoke immediately poured into the air.

A group of beavers in the queue shrieked: "It's on fire!"

One of the London Eye staff whipped out a walkie-talkie and started shouting into it.

Three seconds later, the London Eye had ground to a halt and an announcement crackled out of a loudspeaker: "One of the generators appears to have overheated. There is no need for alarm."

The animals in the pods peered down through the glass, looking confused.

Wily hopped over the barrier and strode past the ticket booth. The staff were so busy they didn't see Wily pick up a high-vis jacket.

He put it on and proceeded to climb the London Eye, leaping from one pod to the next. When he got close to the top, he started clambering through the metal struts. In less than a minute, he was under the cabin containing the pigeon and the hooded figure. Inside he could hear the mumble of voices.

He clamped his ear against the metal pod.

"Mrfgh … *Daily Smear*," said one voice.

"Grff … Catalina … mrff," said the other.

The Daily Smear, Wily thought to himself. *Sounds like it* is *Pete in there.*

Wily opened the door on the side of the pod, threw in a smoke pellet and then closed it again.

"That should cause some chaos," he said to himself.

The pod filled with smoke and Wily could hear coughing and snarling inside.

COUGH SNARL COUGH

His plan was to wait ten seconds, then press the emergency door release. He'd be able to catch whoever was in there as they rushed to escape the smoke-filled pod.

But then he heard a strange scraping sound. As he climbed on to the top of the pod to investigate, two animals came flying out.

He pulled the disc from his pocket, pressed the button and watched it expand into a hang-glider, then jumped.

The mystery animal was already a dark speck in the evening sky, but the pigeon was closer. If Wily was quick, he would reach him.

He pulled up the nose of the glider to gain more height. The pigeon was heading for the opposite side of the river. When Wily was directly above the pigeon, he pulled down the nose and dived. The pigeon saw Wily coming and tacked left towards Big Ben and the Houses of Parliament. Wily whistled past the pigeon's tail and had to pull up sharply, skimming the surface of the river. Then Wily swooped under Westminster Bridge and pulled the glider round to the left.

The pigeon was in front of Big Ben, his flapping getting slower. Wily aimed the glider straight at him, hurtling through the air like an arrow. The pigeon tried to change direction, but couldn't turn fast enough. He ended up flying straight into Big Ben's clockface and getting one of his wings jammed under the minute hand.

Wily pulled up, landing gracefully on the hour hand and retracting the hang-glider.

"Have you got a minute?" he said to the trapped pigeon.

"Very comical," said the pigeon in a strong London accent. He tugged at his wing and winced in pain. "My editor ain't going to like this. We're supposed to report the story, not BE the story." He peered down at the crowd of animals gathered below.

"Listen, Pete," Wily said.

"How do you know my name?"

"I didn't. I suspected," Wily said, "and you've just confirmed it. I'll let you go if you answer my questions."

"Who are you? Police?" asked the pigeon.

"No. Your answers won't go any further than this giant grandfather clock. Ready?"

Pete Pigeon tugged at his wing again and sighed. "Don't have much choice, do I? OK, get your skates on before some joker with a telephoto lens puts me on the front page."

"Who were you meeting at the London Eye?" asked Wily.

"I don't know his name."

"What kind of animal was he?"

"I don't know."

"What did he look like?"

"I don't know. He had a hood on."

"You can't tell me ANYTHING about him?"

"When he shook my wing to greet me, he nearly ripped it off. His hand was like a hook. Now please help me off this thing."

"Not so fast. Why were you meeting him?"

Pete sighed. "He was going to give me another story. Yesterday, he gave me the lowdown on the Griffin Theatre being haunted.

This time, he said he had an even better one. About some private-eye fox fella being scared to death by the same ghost. He said— Hang on a mo! That's YOU, isn't it?"

Pete squinted and pointed at Wily with his free wing.

Wily smiled. "Might be. Listen, I want you to print that story. Then I'll let you go."

"You want me to print it?"

"Yes. Write that we had a tussle on Big Ben, but that you escaped. I don't want him to know that you told me ANYTHING."

"And if I agree to this, you'll let me go?"

Wily nodded.

"Fair enough," said Pete, and held out his free wing for Wily to shake.

"Two more questions," Wily said. "Who's Catalina? Your friend mentioned her."

"I don't know," said Pete. "At the end,

he said he had to call Catalina Covasna. I said, 'Who's she when she's at home?' and he looked surprised. Then he laughed and said: 'Oh, you don't need to worry about HER.'"

"Curious," said Wily. "OK, final question. How did you get out of the pod?"

"Search me," said Pete. "It was full of smoke, wasn't it? I heard scraping and clicking and then the door was open. I took my chance and hopped it."

Wily eased Pete's wing out from under the minute hand and watched him fly away.

What's our villain up to? They don't usually want publicity. So why is this one talking to a journalist? Wily thought.

He pressed the button to expand the hang-glider, jumped off the clockface and headed back to update Albert, the chimes of Big Ben echoing behind him.

THE EMPTY OFFICE

The following morning, Wily was in Albert's laboratory, on a video call with Roderick Rabbit.

"I'm certain it wasn't a ghost," Wily said. "It's some crook in a costume. He haunted your theatre and then told the newspapers."

"So the leak didn't come from one of my actors?" Roderick asked anxiously.

"That I'm not sure of," Wily said. "It's still not clear who or WHAT the villain is."

"This is dreadful," Roderick gasped. "It's Thursday morning. I need to open again on

Saturday and you've no idea who's doing this."

Once again, tears formed in Roderick's tiny eyes.

"Don't worry, we've got plenty of amazing clues," Wily said. "We're THIS CLOSE to solving the case." Wily held up his finger and thumb, indicating a tiny gap. He said goodbye to Roderick and hung up.

"How many amazing clues do we actually have?" Albert asked Wily.

"Er ... none," Wily said. He glanced down at his notebook. "All of our clues are dead ends," he continued. "We know the creature has a hook for a hand, but lots of animals have talons and it might even have been a fake hand. We know that the animal can fly, but he could also be using a contraption like our hang-glider. We know he can open any door – including the doors on the London Eye, but we're not sure how. We know he can turn himself into a ghost, but we haven't found a costume. He has a high-pitched shriek, but we're not sure how he's producing it."

"It is very mysterious," Albert nodded.

"You've been keeping track of all the actors in Roderick's company?" Wily asked.

"Yes," said Albert. "They've done nothing suspicious."

"Have you examined the glowing fabric I found on the stage?" Wily asked.

"Yes, it's cotton that's been treated with Glo-fix 7," Albert said. "The most fluorescent chemical in the world. You need access to a laboratory to create the compound – but thousands of animals will have that."

"Another dead end … for now," Wily said. "OK, we've got two clues left. When the villain spoke to Pete Pigeon, he mentioned Catalina Covasna. Can you run a criminal records check for anyone with that name?"

"Will do," said Albert.

"Lastly, the hotel brochure that the villain dropped. Did you look into the company – Hapgood Hotels?"

Albert frowned, bringing up a password screen on his computer. "I didn't get far. They have an extremely high level of security. I can't hack into their guest records. I've tried every trick in the book."

Wily grinned. "EVERY trick?"

Albert sighed. "What are you going to do?"

"Look – we think our villain might be staying at one of their hotels and I don't have any other leads."

"True," said Albert.

"So I'm going to check in," said Wily, "and check *them* out."

Albert frowned. "You're not going to break the law, are you, Wily?"

Wily fished out a pair of glasses and a fake moustache from his inside pocket. "Certainly not. Just trying out a new look."

He put on his disguise and went over to a trampoline in the corner of Albert's lab.

He climbed on to it and bounced once, twice, three times. On the third bounce, the elastic achieved optimum springiness and shot Wily directly upwards like a rocket. He hurtled up a dark shaft at lightning speed. When he reached the top of it, he clapped his paws and a manhole cover flipped open above his head. He sprang out into the air, emerging into a deserted side alley and landing on a carefully positioned pile of cardboard boxes.

Stepping down on to the ground, he said, "Better jump to it."

He looked up "Hapgood Hotels, Head Office" on his spyphone and a red dot appeared next to a large building about a mile away. The guest database would be in that building somewhere. And perhaps it would contain the name of Wily's ghost.

Wily arrived at the office of Hapgood Hotels at nine o'clock – fifteen minutes later. It was closed. He took off his disguise and rapped on the door. Nobody appeared.

Then he noticed a sign on the window.

Of course, Wily thought, *the hotels are aimed at nocturnal animals. So their office opens in the evening and closes in the morning.*

Then a smile crossed Wily's face. *That means everyone who works here is at home.*

He looked up and down the street. A couple of animals were chatting on the other side of the road, but otherwise it was empty. He pulled out his spyphone and held it against the door handle. Albert had built him an app that could unlock any door – it had something to do with magnets and photons. Wily heard the levers and tumblers clicking, then the door swung open.

Wily ducked in and closed the blinds so nobody could see him. Then he got to work.

First, the filing cabinet. It was full of financial documents, but he couldn't see anything obviously suspicious.

Then he inspected the noticeboard. At the top, there was a banner saying "Meet the Team" with photos of various animals below it. The boss was called Bartholomew Bat – he was a cheerful-looking fruit bat wearing a shiny cape. His secretary was called Bruno Badger – he wore large tinted glasses – and the chief accountant was called Arlene Aardvark – she had an eye patch and a deep scar on her chin. There were also two sales assistants – Oscar Ocelot and Paulo Possum.

All nocturnal animals, of course. And Wily
was sure he'd seen Arlene Aardvark before.
Wily took photos of the noticeboard and
moved across to the desk.

In the top drawer, there was a photo with a
Post-it note stuck to it.

Wily took a picture of this, too.

Then he got to work on the computer. He tried all of his usual techniques to bypass the password screen, but none of them worked. Albert was right. Their security system was top of the range. This was common on military bases and in government offices, but unusual for a hotel chain.

But Wily wasn't about to give up. "Everyone – EVERYONE – writes their password down somewhere," he mumbled.

He glanced around the rest of the office and saw another picture. It was an oil painting of the owner, Bartholomew Bat, standing with one of his wings resting on a giant globe.

Only one reason for a painting like that, Wily thought. He slid it sideways and, sure enough, there was a small wall-safe behind it. *There you are!* Wily thought to himself. He held up

his spyphone against the combination lock.
It spun left, then right and then popped open.
Inside there was a bundle of banknotes and a
large black book. On the first page of the book
was a list of symbols.

Wily smiled. It was a pretty basic code. In
The Case of the Cunning Vixen, he'd had to
crack one hundred and nine different codes in
less than five minutes while being suspended
over a bath full of piranhas. So this one was
child's play.

In fifteen seconds, he had all the computer passwords. He typed in one password to unlock the computer, then another to access the guest database.

Hundreds of names filled the screen. Ferrets, cats, lorises, hedgehogs, hamsters – every nocturnal animal in the world.

"Albert," Wily said into his spyphone, "I'm sending you the London guest list. Start with the animals that are in London right now. Then move on to the animals that stayed last week. Then look at other hotels in Europe."

A few names leaped out at Wily – Otto Owl, Patsy Pangolin, Casper Kite.

"Start with the animals who have wings, talons or both," said Wily.

"Will do," Albert said. "Now get out of there. You've broken about fifty laws in the past ten minutes."

"It's OK," said Wily, "nobody will ever..."

His voice trailed off. He was looking straight ahead. How had he been so foolish? He'd been so focused on taking photos with HIS camera that he'd forgotten about THEIR camera. There it was, above the door. Pointing directly at him.

Wily stepped to the left. The camera moved slightly to the left. Wily stepped to the right. The camera swivelled right. It had a motion sensor. It must have recorded every move he'd made.

"Albert," said Wily, "we may have the smallest smidgen of a problem."

"Uh-oh," said Albert.

Wily tapped frantically into the computer. Could he

find the security camera files? He tried all the obvious folders, but they were empty.

"It's just that…" Wily mumbled.

"It's just that … what?" Albert replied.

Wily ran a search for any file that had been created today. *At last!* Video files with today's date. But when he tried to delete them, a message popped up. "This will only delete local versions." What did that mean? Wily tapped the "info" button and discovered that the security files were all backed up on to remote servers in California and Mumbai. *Blast!* There were copies everywhere – all of them impossible to delete.

"Er, well," Wily continued, "when the staff come back to the office at 6 p.m. tonight, they MIGHT find out I've been here."

"How?" Albert asked, panic in his voice.

"I kind of … got caught on camera."

"Wily! I told you to be careful. This is a catastrophe!"

"I know, I know," Wily said, "but it just adds to the fun. It means we've got to solve the case by 6 p.m. this evening. Piece of cake!"

"But … but…" Albert stammered, "it'll take me a while to check these names against the criminal database. There's not enough TIME!"

Wily walked round the desk, the camera following him as he moved.

"You can do it, Albert," said Wily. "Someone on that guest list may well be our ghost. I'm coming back to the lab."

Suddenly Wily heard a click and the office door opened. He instantly dived behind the desk. Peering out from underneath it, he saw the feet of two animals – a bat and an aardvark.

"Thanks for coming in early, Arlene," the bat said. "I need your help with the new catalogue."

"You're welcome, Mr Bat, sir," Arlene replied.

It appeared to be the owner – Bartholomew Bat – and his assistant, Arlene Aardvark.

Wily had to think fast. He looked around and spotted a red button under the desk: Intruder Alarm.

He pressed it. A loud wailing tore through the air and a light on the ceiling started to flash.

"Oh no, we must have tripped the alarm!" Bartholomew exclaimed.

While the two animals were fiddling with a control panel in the corner of the room, Wily slipped out. "Daylight robbery," he murmured, stepping out on to the street.

THE CREEPY CASTLE

Wily was heading across London on his hang-glider, talking to Albert on his headset.

"So now we have even LESS time to solve the case," Albert said, sounding more stressed than ever.

"Afraid so," said Wily. "Once they've looked through those security tapes, they'll send them straight to the police. I wouldn't be surprised if Julius and Sybil were on their way to our office now. That's why I'm not coming back to HQ."

Detective Julius Hound and Sergeant Sybil Squirrel worked for PSSST – the Police Spy, Sleuth and Snoop Taskforce. Julius and Wily didn't exactly get on – they often ended up investigating the same cases, and Wily usually solved them first.

"Where are you going?" Albert asked.

"That depends on what you've found out," Wily said. "Have you discovered anything suspicious about the hotel's guests?"

"Not yet," said Albert, "but I've only checked the birds of prey so far."

"OK," said Wily, looking down at central London. "What about the villain's friend – Catalina Covasna?"

"I've been looking for her, too," said Albert. "She didn't show up in the criminal records database."

"Hmm," Wily muttered.

Wily steered his hang-glider right across
Soho. He passed Warren Street and then Russell
Square. A thought dropped into his head. *Don't
places sometimes sound like people?* A foreigner
might not know whether Warren Street was a
person or a place.

Then he thought about what Pete had
said: the villain was going to "call Catalina
Covasna". When Wily was on cases abroad, he
often talked about calling London.

"Albert," Wily said aloud. "What if Catalina
Covasna is a place?"

Wily heard Albert tapping at his computer.

"You've cracked it!" Albert said. "I've sent you a picture."

Wily looked at his phone. Catalina was a small village in Romania in the region of Covasna.

"And look at this news report," Albert said.

BUCHAREST BUGLE

HUNTING IN CATALINA
by Winnie Wolf

One of Romania's oldest buildings — Catalina Castle — has been sold following the appearance of a ghastly ghoul. The ghost was seen by Baron Berbatov and his wife, Olga, while they were sleeping in the castle's master bedroom last month.

Olga Berbatov described "a white shrouded figure with red eyes that seemed to float above the ground". The Baron described the piercing shriek the ghost made.

"It looks like our villain might have done this before," Wily said. "And I wonder who he was calling there? Time for a trip to Romania, I think. After what happened at the Hapgood office, I need to leave town anyway."

"Sure thing, Wily," said Albert.

"In the meantime, keep looking through those hotel records," said Wily. "I'll call when I get to Romania."

"Oh yes, about that," Albert said. "I wasn't going to tell you this, but…"

"What is it?" Wily asked.

Albert sighed. "The control bar of your hang-glider has a purple button underneath it. Press that twice and you'll go at the speed of sound. I haven't tested it properly yet, but—"

"Bravo, Albert!" Wily said. "If Roderick calls while I'm away, tell him to start selling tickets for Saturday. And save me a seat in the front row."

Wily felt for the button under the control bar and pressed it twice. He zipped forwards at the speed of sound, the wind blowing his ears flat.

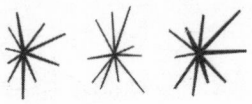

As Wily flew, he went through the case in his head. There was some connection he wasn't making. The glowing paint. The claw. The way the ghost could open all doors. The fact it was a nocturnal animal. Above all, what did it have against Roderick Rabbit? Wily hoped he'd find answers in Catalina Castle.

As he glided towards Catalina, he saw three of the castle's turrets poking through the clouds. He swooped down, expecting to see a beautiful Gothic building, but as he emerged from the clouds he saw that all four walls were covered with scaffolding. He flew closer and saw a giant "DANGER – KEEP OUT" sign tied to a pole.

He landed on the scaffolding and a rabbit's head immediately appeared at the top of a ladder.

"I'm sorry, mate," the rabbit said, "but you can't park your contraption here – this is a building site."

DANGER - KEEP OUT

Wily put on an exaggerated American accent. "I sure am sorry, sir. The name's Arnold J. Dingleberry III. I'm in Romania on vacation. I was hoping to mosey on into this here castle."

"Well, you can't," said the rabbit. "The owners sold it."

"And why is that, sir?"

The rabbit swallowed and looked over his shoulder. "On account of the ghost. They had to sell it for next to nothing, too – nobody wanted to buy a haunted castle."

At that moment, another rabbit's head appeared at the top of the ladder. He was older, and he had grey fur and a chipped front tooth.

"Who are you talking to, Ricky? What have you said?" the old rabbit barked.

"He's just a tourist," Ricky gibbered.

"How many times? We've promised not to say anything about why we're here."

The old rabbit looked up at Wily.

"You need to get out of here and never come back."

"Why, certainly," Wily said with a small bow. He took off and landed on the other side of the castle.

OK, Wily thought to himself, *how am I going to get inside? I need to find out what's been going on here.*

It was around four in the afternoon. The builders would probably start to go home shortly. He decided to wait until they headed off, then break in.

He looked up at the castle. What was the connection between this and the Griffin Theatre in London? Had the same ghost haunted both buildings? And why?

Within half an hour, the coast was clear and Wily was scaling the scaffolding. He found an

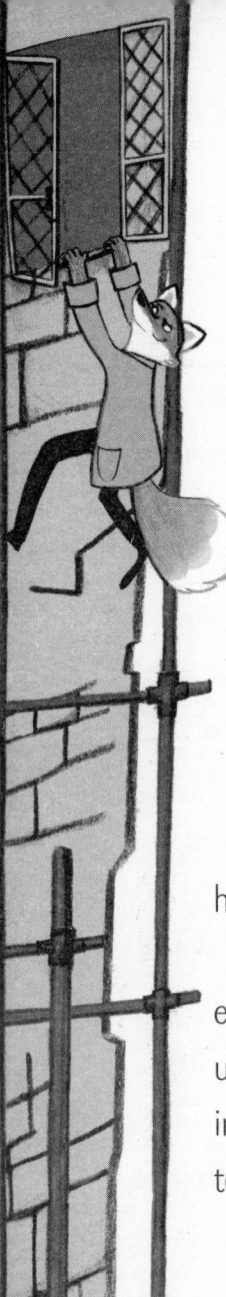

open window and climbed inside.

He remembered the news article: "The ghost was seen by Baron Berbatov and his wife, Olga, while they were sleeping in the castle's master bedroom."

He needed to find the master bedroom and look for clues.

Tricky, Wily said to himself, *when half the castle is a building site.*

He walked through the old dining room. There was a cloth thrown over the long dining table and one of the walls had been knocked down.

Wily opened the double doors at the end of the room and found himself in what used to be a study. It had been converted into the foreman's office – it was full of tools and overalls and documents.

Wily noticed several large sheets of

paper laid out on a desk in the centre of the office. They were architectural plans showing the castle before and after the building works.

I'll ask Albert to decipher all these numbers and measurements, Wily said to himself, taking photographs of each plan.

Then he moved out of the office and into the hall. He climbed up a large staircase and opened the door directly in front of him. It was a bedroom. It still had a four-poster bed at one end and a chest of drawers at the other.

The master bedroom, Wily thought.

He got down on all fours and looked for clues, sniffing the air and inspecting the carpet. Then he saw something glinting in the corner of the room. He dashed over and saw a twist of fabric under the chest of drawers. In the darkness, he could see it glowing faintly. When he pulled it out, the fabric turned black. It looked identical

to the material that he'd found at the Griffin
Theatre. Glo-fix 7, Albert had called it.

Wily smiled. "What a spooky coincidence,"
he said.

The next second, his smile vanished.

"Hands up!" said a stern voice behind him.

Quick as a flash, Wily reached into his
pocket for the particle freezer and shot it
between his legs.

Then he spun round.

Detective Julius Hound of PSSST was
standing in the doorway, frozen solid.

His deputy, Sybil Squirrel, was
standing in front of him. She
broke into a smile.

"Wily!" she exclaimed.
"What are YOU doing
in Romania?"

THE SECRET PASSAGE

"Sybil!" Wily exclaimed. "I could ask you the same question."

"We were in Bucharest," Sybil said, "investigating a lead that went nowhere. Then we got a call saying that Mad Vlad the Killer Gorilla was holed up in Catalina Castle. He's Romania's most wanted criminal. We were close by, so we decided to come in person."

"That's strange," said Wily. "One of the builders must have seen me breaking in. But why did they lie and tell you I was a murderer?

They must be desperate to get rid of me. Perhaps they're worried I'll find the link to the ghost."

"Ghost?" Sybil said. "What ghost?"

Wily gave Sybil a brief description of his case. When he'd finished, he said, "I found glowing fabric under that chest of drawers. Now I'm going to look for more clues. I need to find out who's behind these fake hauntings."

Wily glanced behind Sybil and asked, "Do you want me to unfreeze your boss?"

Sybil looked over her shoulder and leaped in surprise.

"Crikey, I thought he was being a bit quiet. Assumed he was having a sulk. What did you do to him?"

"Nothing serious," said Wily. "I just froze every particle in his body."

He pressed the "thaw" button.

As Julius started to unfreeze, Wily said, "By the way, Sybil, did Hapgood Hotels contact PSSST?"

Sybil looked blank. "Not that I heard of."

"They didn't report an office break-in?"

Sybil pulled out her phone and typed something into it. "Nope. Not to us or any other police agency. Why?"

"Because I broke into their office," said Wily, "and I'm wondering why they didn't tell anyone."

There were so many strands to this case. Wily knew everything was linked, but he couldn't see how – yet.

His train of thought was interrupted when Julius exclaimed, "Blasted fox!" and threw an empty paint pot at Wily.

Wily blocked it and the paint pot rebounded, hitting Julius on the head and knocking him backwards. Julius grabbed one of the posts of the four-poster bed and, trying to regain his balance, twisted it.

Something creaked in the wall behind them.

"Julius, do that again," Wily said.

Julius looked confused so Wily walked across to the bed and twisted the bedpost. A panel opened in the wall at the other end of the room.

Wily looked at Julius and then at the secret passage that had just been revealed.

"Julius!" he cried. "You may have just solved my case!"

"*Your* case!" Julius exclaimed. "If there's a case to be solved, it belongs to me. And you're under arrest for trespassing."

"Catch me if you can," Wily said, dashing towards the secret passage.

Sybil ran after him. Julius tried to follow, then realized that his right foot wasn't completely thawed. He ran as fast as he could, dragging his partly frozen foot behind him.

Sybil caught up with Wily and said, "I really SHOULD arrest you, you know."

Wily smiled and took out his torch, shining it into the gloom. "The ghost must have used these passages to move around the castle."

They found themselves crawling under a low beam and then climbing a narrow set of stairs. They emerged into a small room at the top of the castle's highest turret.

Wily could see clothes, documents and tools. He grinned. Somewhere in this room, he'd find the answers he needed – who was the ghost? Why had it haunted the Griffin Theatre?

Wily looked more closely at the room's contents. There were steel rings attached to one of the walls – had the room formerly been used as a dungeon? There was also a metal bar stretched across one corner of the room. It was screwed into the wall, about two metres from the ground. Underneath the metal bar was a pair of pyjamas. Wily picked them up and saw that the bottoms had elasticated ankles. That was odd. With pyjama bottoms, it was usually the waist that was elasticated.

"Wily, over here," Sybil said. "It's an address book," she said, "full of journalists' names."

Wily read:

Roberto Rhino, The Roman Chronicle:
   0777 3342 123
Sergio Sloth, The Buenos Aires Daily:
   0555 5656 565
Winnie Wolf, The Bucharest Bugle:
   0758 6222 334
Pete Pigeon, The Daily Smear:
   0888 2333 445

"Winnie Wolf," Wily murmured. "She wrote the story about the castle haunting."

"But why would a ghost want to tell journalists what he was doing?" Sybil asked.

"And what's the connection with Rome and Buenos Aires?" Wily added.

Wily walked over to the window, his brain

buzzing. *What's the connection? Why can't I see the bigger picture?*

He looked out of the window and everything clicked.

The PICTURE.

There, on the opposite side of the valley, was a town with all of its lights blazing. He whipped out his phone and found the photo of the brochure that he'd taken in the Hapgood Hotels office.

"That's it!" he cried.

He phoned Albert.

"Albert, it's me!" Wily said urgently. "Have you checked all the Hapgood guests?"

"Yes, but I've come up with nothing."

"Forget the guests," Wily said, "check the STAFF."

"The staff?"

"Arlene Aardvark, Bruno Badger, the whole lot of them. The photo for their new brochure was taken in this castle."

Wily said goodbye to Albert and hung up.

"Have you solved the case?" Sybil asked.

"Almost," Wily said. "I think I've worked out WHY the villain haunted the Griffin Theatre. He wants to transform it into a hotel. Roderick Rabbit and Vladimir Vole were just in the way. He did the same here. He haunted the building and it got a reputation for being cursed.

The owners put it up for sale, but nobody wanted to buy it. So they sold it for a knockdown price to Hapgood Hotels."

"But hang on," said Sybil. "Isn't that a bit risky? Who'd want to stay in a haunted hotel?"

"Nocturnal animals," said Wily.

"I don't follow," she said.

"They're not afraid of the dark, are they?" Wily said. "They LOVE the dark. Because they're up all night, they know that ghosts aren't real. The fact that a building used to be haunted wouldn't bother them."

At that point, Julius appeared.

"OK, Fox," he barked. "Give me one good reason why I shouldn't throw this at your head."

Wily glanced at the bottle in Julius's hand. It was glowing faintly in the darkness.

"Julius, where did you find that?"

"I thought YOU were supposed to be the

great detective," Julius sneered. "It was in a concealed panel in the master bedroom. I was using it as a torch."

"Is there anything written on the bottle?" asked Wily.

Julius reluctantly held it up. The label on the side read "Glo-fix 7".

"The final piece of the puzzle," murmured Wily.

"The final piece?" Julius snarled. "What's the puzzle, then? Where's the criminal?"

"In London," said Wily, "working for Hapgood Hotels."

"Not good enough," barked Julius. "Your ghost story doesn't make sense." He clicked a handcuff on Wily's wrist and attached the other cuff to one of the metal rings that hung from the wall. "You're under arrest – and this time you're staying that way."

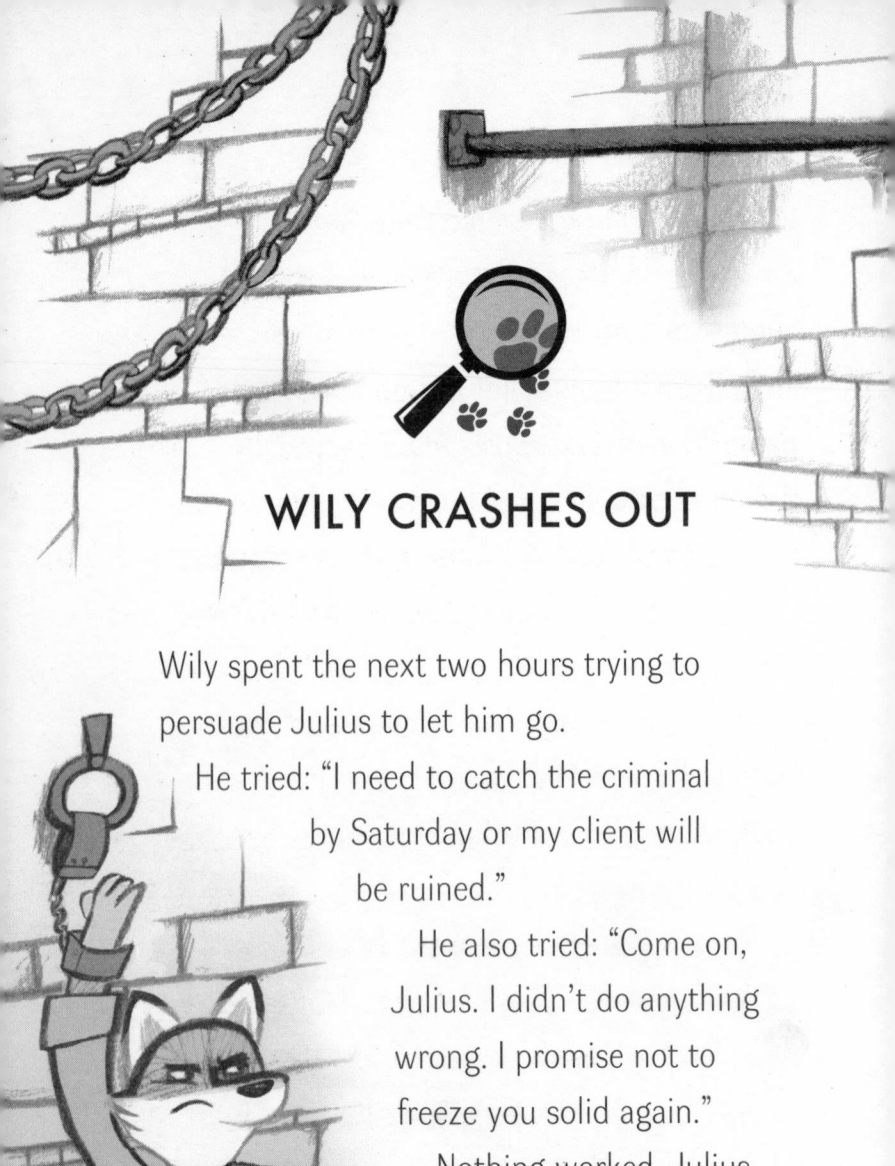

WILY CRASHES OUT

Wily spent the next two hours trying to persuade Julius to let him go.

He tried: "I need to catch the criminal by Saturday or my client will be ruined."

He also tried: "Come on, Julius. I didn't do anything wrong. I promise not to freeze you solid again."

Nothing worked. Julius had called for a PSSST

helicopter and they weren't moving until it arrived. In the meantime, Wily was thinking about the case. He went through all the animals that worked for Hapgood Hotels. *Badgers, aardvarks, possums...* Eventually tiredness overwhelmed him and he dozed off.

He was shaken awake by an almighty crash.

Sybil raced to the window and yelled, "The workers are here – with a wrecking ball!" There was another crash. "They must be knocking down the tower!"

She shouted to the workers below, but they were too far away to hear.

"Uncuff me from the wall!" Wily shouted.

"No way, Fox," Julius said. "I'm not falling for your tricks."

"What tricks?" Wily yelled. "The tower's falling down and they don't know we're here!"

"You stay there while I give those workers a

piece of my mind," Julius barked. He sped off down the secret passage.

Wily turned to Sybil. "He'll never get to them in time. You've got to uncuff me."

Sybil looked over her shoulder to check Julius was gone, then whipped out her keys and undid the handcuffs.

As Wily put the cuffs in his pocket, the crane whacked into the tower again, knocking Sybil and Wily to the ground.

"Let's try and put a stop to this," Wily said, getting back to his feet.

He ran to the window and pulled out his particle freezer. He aimed it at the animal in the crane. A blue streak jumped from the end of the gun, but it fizzled to nothing in mid-air.

"He's too far away," Wily said. He put his hand in his pocket. "OK, here's my second plan. I've got a hang-glider, but I think it will be too heavy for both of us."

He threw Sybil the disc. "You take it. Press the middle and it will spring to life."

Sybil looked down at the disc and up at Wily. "I'm not going without you," she said.

There was an ear-splitting crack, lumps of plaster fell down from the ceiling and Wily and Sybil were knocked over again.

They scrambled back to their feet. "I reckon it will take one more swing to knock the turret over," Wily said. "We haven't got time to argue. You take the hang-glider, I'll try to jump."

"No," said Sybil. "I'll jump, too."

"Don't be silly," said Wily. "There's no point two of us breaking our legs."

Sybil folded her arms and said, "Either we both get on the hang-glider or we both jump."

"You've made up your mind?" said Wily.

"I've made up my mind," said Sybil.

They both stared out of the window at the ground far below.

Wily glanced at his particle freezer again. "I've got an idea," he said.

He held the hang-glider disc out of the window and pressed the button in the centre. Then he grabbed Sybil's hand and leaped on to the hang-glider just as the wrecking ball hit the turret. The tower started to fall and the hang-glider dived towards the ground, with the falling tower hurtling after them.

"Hang on!" said Wily.

He turned the particle freezer round so it was facing behind him, then he set it to "thaw". The rush of hot air acted like a blaster, sending the hang-glider forwards into the sky.

They soared upwards, past the confused-looking crane operator and over the forest around the castle.

"What about Julius?" Sybil asked anxiously.

They glanced over their shoulders and saw a bulldog's head emerge from the rubble, shouting. One of the workmen tried to pull Julius out, but ended up dislodging another pile of rocks and burying him again.

"He'll be fine," said Wily. He hit "thaw" on the particle freezer, sending out more hot air and rocketing them higher into the sky.

"How long to get back to London?" Sybil asked.

"An hour or so," said Wily. "Time to work out who my ghost is."

"I have to say," Sybil said, "I can't make sense of any of the clues. Upside-down pyjamas. Luminous chemicals. And your ghost with claws for hands and a high-pitched shriek. It's hard to see any connection."

"What did you just say?" Wily replied.

"I said, it's hard to see any connection."

"It's hard to see ... it's hard to see ... IT'S HARD TO SEE! Of course!" He gave Sybil a kiss on the cheek.

"The animal finds it hard to see!" Wily cried. "When he first attacked me, he used a cane to help him get around. We know he's nocturnal. We think he can fly. He has talons for hands. Then there's the pole attached to the wall.

His pyjamas were below it. That's where he sleeps ... UPSIDE DOWN. Sybil, he's a bat!"

Wily phoned Albert immediately. "Bartholomew Bat – the head of Hapgood Hotels. Focus all your attention on him," said Wily. "Where's he from? Is he who he says he is?"

"OK – but why?" Albert asked.

"He's my prime suspect," said Wily. "He covers himself in glowing paint to appear like a ghost. He uses his high-pitched shriek to scare people. Then when everyone is frightened off, his hotel chain buy the building. He's done it here in Catalina, and now he's trying to do it at the Griffin Theatre, too!"

"It sounds possible," said Albert.

"It's either him or another bat," said Wily, "but I reckon it's him. Think about it. And that explains how he's managed to unlock so many

doors. He got into the Griffin Theatre. And into
Vladimir's dressing room. He got out of the
London Eye cabin. He must have a key for every
kind of door. In the hotel business, you need
passkeys and service keys and skeleton keys."

"OK, I'll check him out."

"We're about to cross the Romanian
border," Wily said. "We'll be with you in less
than an hour."

He hung up and turned to face Sybil.

But just as he was about to speak, he heard a
whoosh from the ground below. They were above
a large forest. A cloud of bats rose into the air.

"Blast! We've got company," said Wily.

"When will they get to us?" Sybil asked.

A bat dropped down in front of them.
"We're already here," he hissed in a thick
Romanian accent.

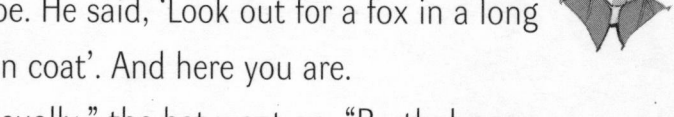

"Let me guess," Wily said, "a friend of Bartholomew Bat?"

"How did you know?" the bat said. "He said that you might show up. He received a phone call last night saying that a strange fox had been seen on his property in Catalina. He called the police, but he thought you might escape. He said, 'Look out for a fox in a long brown coat'. And here you are.

"Usually," the bat went on, "Bartholomew is a businessman. If people get in his way, he prefers to warn or frighten them away. But he wants you gone… For good."

As he said "good", the bat grinned, revealing two sharp fangs.

"A vampire bat," Sybil shuddered.

The bat spun sideways and tore a rip in the top of Wily's hang-glider with his fangs.

The wind fluttered through it and the hang-glider started to wobble violently.

"Prepare for landing," the bat hissed.

Wily tried to grab his particle freezer, but he needed both hands to steer the glider.

The other bats from the forest had now arrived. One of them whipped past and made another tear in the hang-glider's fabric. Wily and Sybil were starting to drop.

Bats were whirling above and below them in wide, shrieking circles.

The chief bat prepared to dive for one final attack on Wily's glider, but as he did so, Wily fumbled for the particle freezer, grabbed it

and swung it round. He pointed it at the bat
and fired. A blue flash zipped over the bat's
shoulder.

"Missed," sneered the chief bat.

"Oh no, I didn't," said Wily.

The bat looked up and saw that Wily had
hit the cloud above him. It had turned into a
giant block of ice and was thundering through
the air. Wily pulled the glider back as the ice
block hit the chief bat and his friends, pulling
them down. Wily watched the cloud plummet,
smashing into pieces on the ground below like
a giant chandelier.

Wily fired at two more clouds, which also
crashed down, taking out more of the bats.

The hang-glider was still just about
airborne, but Wily needed to repair it fast. And
it looked like the battle with the bats wasn't
over yet.

"Wily," said Sybil, "there's one left."

Wily saw a small shape zooming towards them, its fangs bared.

Wily blasted it with his particle freezer, but the bat simply dodged it.

"Ow," said Sybil. The bat had locked on to her arm and was trying to drink her blood!

Wily lashed out and knocked the bat sideways, but Sybil had turned pale and let go of the hang-glider. She plummeted towards the ground.

The bat was already zipping back towards Wily, its fangs gleaming, aiming for his neck. He suddenly remembered Julius's handcuffs in his pocket. Quick as a flash, he clipped one of the handcuffs round the bat's legs and attached the other cuff to the crossbar.

The bat squealed in anger.

Wily let go of the hang-glider.

"See ya, sucker."

The hang-glider was diving towards the ground and Wily was falling, too. He could see Sybil below him. He put his arms flat against his sides, nosediving towards her.

In a few seconds he caught up, grabbing her round the waist.

She was still semi-conscious, murmuring to herself.

They were hurtling towards a large lake. Wily spotted a waterfall and twisted himself and Sybil to face it. They were a few seconds away from hitting the water.

With lightning speed, Wily aimed the particle freezer at the waterfall and fired, turning it into a giant ice slide. The ice spread down the waterfall and on to the lake, transforming it into a huge ice rink.

Wily braced for impact, curling himself round Sybil. They hit the ice slide with a *whoomph*, slithering down it like they were on the world's fastest sledge. When they reached the bottom, they zoomed across the giant sheet of ice.

A hundred metres away, Wily saw his hang-glider – with the bat attached – dive into the middle of a forest. There was a loud *crunch* and a louder *crash*.

Sybil woke up.

"This case is strange," she said.

Wily nodded. "I know. Completely bats."

THE BAT TRAP

An hour later the PSSST helicopter arrived
in Romania and picked them up. On the trip
back, Sybil persuaded Julius not to arrest Wily.

"He's telling the truth, sir," Sybil said.
"Bartholomew Bat is a big-time criminal."

"I still don't see how you can prove it, Fox,"
Julius said. "You've got clues that point to a
bat haunting a castle, but no definite proof
that it was Bartholomew."

"But those vampire bats…" Sybil began.

"You know we need fingerprints or DNA to

make it stick in court," Julius interrupted.

"How about a confession?" Wily asked.

Julius stared at Wily and then growled, "That would work. I'll give you twenty-four hours to get one."

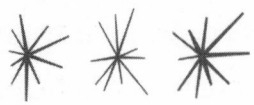

As soon as he got back to London, Wily headed for Albert's lab and studied everything that Albert had found out about Bartholomew. He opened and closed pictures and documents on a giant screen.

"So this is his life story," said Wily.

Albert nodded.

"The story of how Bartholomew took over Hapgood Hotels from his father. His father was a scary character, but Bartholomew looked up to him," Wily said, zooming into a black-and-white photo of a bat with large grey side-whiskers. "Then he got married, but his wife died in a mid-air collision with a kestrel, leaving Bartholomew angry and bitter." Wily clicked on a photo of a young female bat with giant pink eyes.

"He concentrated on his work instead," Wily continued. "He gradually put his rivals out of business. Including his old friend, Billy Bison – who died of a broken heart after his last hotel closed down." A picture of Billy Bison appeared on screen.

"Finally he cooked up this ghost idea.

Finding old buildings that could be turned into hotels. Scaring the owners, then using journalists to tell everyone the buildings were haunted. Then buying them cheap."

"That's about the size of it," Albert said.

"Albert, I know exactly what we need to do," said Wily. "We need to beat him at his own game."

"Open a hotel?" asked Albert.

"No, not that game," said Wily. "The haunting game."

Wily made a video call to Roderick Rabbit. When Roderick appeared on screen, Wily explained who had haunted the Griffin Theatre and why.

"And now we're going to prove it to your actors," said Wily.

"Splendid," said Roderick.

"But we'll need their help," Wily added.

"They're going to put on the greatest ghost story ever."

"Marvellous," said Roderick. "What's it called?"

"The Haunting of Bartholomew Bat," said Wily. "Vladimir Vole will be the ghost of Bartholomew's father. Gloria Gerbil will be the ghost of his wife. We'll also need some actors to play Bartholomew's dead friends. Bring along lots of make-up and stage lighting."

He gave Roderick the rest of the details and then hung up. Next he put on a giant curly wig and stuck a twirly moustache to his top lip. He called the Hapgood Hotels head office. Arlene Aardvark appeared on screen.

"I weesh to speek to Bartholomew Bat and only heem," Wily said in a thick French accent.

"Mr Bat is asleep," Arlene said. "It's the middle of the night for him."

"This deal could earn heem millions of Eenglish pounds," Wily said.

Arlene disappeared and thirty seconds later, Bartholomew appeared in a night cap.

"OK, who are you and what's this about?" Bartholomew yawned.

For a couple of seconds, Wily stared at Bartholomew. He was finally face to face with his adversary. Like most fruit bats, Bartholomew had large brown eyes that flickered red from certain angles.

"*Non!*" Wily exclaimed. "I explain notheeng through a screen. We meet. I 'ave a graveyard next to the Thames. St John's in Limehouse. You know eet? Well, I want to sell eet."

Bartholomew's large eyes narrowed in

suspicion. "This is a con," he said.

"Fine. You don't want eet, I sell it to Merrygreen Hotels instead."

This seemed to work. Bartholomew gritted his teeth in distaste.

"So," Wily went on, "meet me at my graveyard at seven o'clock tonight and bring 'alf a million pounds. Or don't. Ees your decision."

Wily hung up and yanked off his wig and moustache. He was certain he'd said enough to make Bartholomew come. Yes, the bat would be suspicious. Yes, he'd probably bring a friend or two with him. But he'd be curious about this French stranger and he wouldn't want to lose out on the deal of the century.

"Bring along every video camera you have," Wily said to Albert. "This is going to be a night to remember."

THE FINAL CURTAIN

It was six o'clock in the evening and the sun was setting over St John's graveyard on the banks of the River Thames. Wily was standing next to a crypt surrounded by the cast of *Escape from Spooky Manor.* They were all made up as ghosts, zombies and skeletons.

Roderick Rabbit stepped forwards. "So, darlings – you understand what's about to happen?"

"We're going to frighten the animal that tried to frighten us!" Vladimir Vole exclaimed.

"We're going to show him how REAL actors put on a horror show," said Gloria Gerbil.

Roderick grinned and a tear welled up in his eye. "That's right. Now, I'm NOT going to cry. But I'm so proud of you all."

All the actors hugged each other.

Wily cleared his throat. "Ahem, we'd better take up our positions. He'll be here soon."

"Of course, Mr Fox. Two minutes till curtain up!"

The actors all scattered: some hid behind gravestones, some in bushes.

Wily tapped the binoculars app on his spyphone and glanced around the cemetery. He spotted Albert in a tree, setting up one of his cameras. Then – there at the entrance – he saw Bartholomew Bat and Arlene Aardvark.

Wily turned on his headset. Albert had placed microphones everywhere, so Wily could hear.

"So, do you think this is genuine, sir?"
Arlene said.

"I'm not sure," said Bartholomew, "but if it
is, we could make a fortune. Putting a giant
hotel on this graveyard would be stupendous.
Right on the banks of the river."

"You don't suspect that fox detective of
being involved?"

"Oh, I suspect him all right," said
Bartholomew. "But I'm pretty sure my cousin
Vlad took care of him in Romania."

Wily made a hooting noise, like an owl. This
was Roderick's cue to start the show.

Vladimir Vole emerged from a tomb in

front of Bartholomew Bat. He was dressed as
Bartholomew's father, complete with large
cape and whiskers.

"Bartholomew," he wailed. "What have you
done…?"

"F-father?" gibbered Bartholomew Bat,
taking a step backwards.

Arlene grabbed Bartholomew's arm.

"I prided myself on running an honest business," said Vladimir, "but YOU. Scaring animals out of their wits. Then buying their property cheap."

"B-but I wanted you to be proud of me," said Bartholomew, "by making the business successful."

"I don't want THAT kind of success," hissed Vladimir. "I'm ashamed of you."

Using a remote control, Vladimir activated a state-of-the-art smoke machine that was hidden in a bush next to him. Plumes of smoke emerged. Then Vladimir appeared to vanish.

Bartholomew seemed to snap out of it. "What am I thinking?" He ran into the tomb but there was nobody there.

"I'm sure that was an actor," he said. "I've used tricks like that myself."

Arlene was looking scared. "Are you s-sure

that w-wasn't a ghost? And what did he m-mean? You b-buying up property cheap?"

"Lies," said Bartholomew. "That wasn't my father's ghost, I'm sure of it. Come on, we need to leave."

But as he walked back towards the exit, his path was blocked by Gloria Gerbil dressed as the ghost of Bartholomew's wife.

"M-Muriel," muttered Bartholomew. But this time, he looked angry rather than scared. He ran up to Gloria and tried to grab her, growling, "This is a trick."

But his hand passed through air. It was a hologram of Gloria beamed into the air by a carefully placed projector. She was actually standing behind a tree right next to the hologram.

"You used to be a good man, a kind man," Gloria said. "What has made you so cruel?"

"I-I try n-not to be cruel," Bartholomew stammered, as if he were in a trance, "it's not like I hurt anyone. I just scare them. Then buy their land."

"You'd better come with me," Gloria moaned, stretching out her arms.

Now Bartholomew was properly scared. He murmured to Arlene, "Run."

Arlene didn't need to be told twice. She vanished, sprinting out of the graveyard, screaming. Bartholomew tried to fly off, but he was too frightened – his wings wouldn't flap. Then he tried to run at the ghost and push it away, but of course he just fell straight through it.

"Come with me now," Gloria continued.

Bartholomew finally managed to flap his wings and took off. But as he rose from the ground, he saw ghosts pouring from every grave – old friends, old family members and old enemies. They groaned and held up their arms towards him.

Bartholomew stopped flapping and dropped to the ground like a stone.

Wily took off his headset and put a white veil over his face. He moved towards where Bartholomew was standing, frozen stiff with fear. He threw smoke pellets in front of him and stood in the centre of a swirl of mist.

"I'm the ghost of Wily Fox," Wily said. "Your cousin killed me in the forests of Romania. And I am here for REVENGE."

This was the last straw for Bartholomew. He spread his wings and took off as fast as he could. But he wasn't alone. Nine ghosts were flying behind him, shrieking and groaning. This was Roderick's final trick. He had brought along jet packs from a production of *Peter Pan*. The rest of the cast were zooming towards Bartholomew, stretching out their hands.

Wily ran down to the river where Sybil and Julius were waiting in a PSSST speedboat.

"You got my message then?" Wily said, hopping on board.

"Yep," Sybil said.

"Try and keep the boat under him," said Wily, "he could drop at any moment."

In the sky above them, Bartholomew was flapping frantically, bouncing off buildings and bridges like a pinball. First, he hit Tower Bridge, then he veered towards the Tower of London. He bumped into Traitor's Gate, then took off again, speeding towards London Bridge. He hit the Shard and then flapped back towards St Paul's, where he smashed off the dome. All the time, the actors dressed as ghouls were just behind him, wailing.

Finally Bartholomew flew across the Thames in a daze, trying to get as high as he could, before whacking into the tall chimney of the Tate Modern and tumbling down towards the river, where Wily and the PSSST speedboat were waiting to catch him.

"Julius, Sybil, take a bow," said Wily – as Bartholomew landed at his feet with a thump.

Wily was standing in his office, feeling distinctly uncomfortable. This is because he was being hugged by Roderick Rabbit.

"OK, you can stop now," Wily said.

"Tonight's performance has SOLD OUT!" Roderick said, continuing to hug Wily. "My play is going to be a SMASH!"

"Just doing my job," Wily said, finally deciding to lift Roderick's arms from round his waist.

"And I'm sure this was your doing, too," Roderick said, handing Wily a newspaper.

Wily took the newspaper and read.

There was a full breakdown of the case.

CHILLING CHASE LEAVES BAT BATTERED
by Pete Pigeon

There were thrilling scenes over the Thames last night as PSSST agents chased and captured vile villain, Bartholomew Bat.

The bat had pretended to be a ghost and haunted the Griffin Theatre during a recent run of *Escape from Spooky Manor*. The brilliant play is now back in business. The bat's goal was to scare everyone away from the building. Then the nocturnal ne'er-do-well planned to buy the land cheap and put up one of his high-class hotels.

"I guess you gave Pete Pigeon an exclusive," said Roderick with a grin.

"Well … I fed him a few crumbs," Wily said.

"So why aren't you mentioned in the article?" Roderick asked. "Don't you want to hog the limelight for once?"

Wily shrugged. "It's better if I stay out of sight. In the shadows."

"You know what you remind me of?"

"What's that?" Wily said.

Roderick smiled. "A ghost."